The Story of Huey Pea

Huey was one of one trillion peas in the world, and was just like other peas, but when Huey was ready to evolve into their next phase of life, Huey was treated uniquely compared to other peas. The story of Huey Pea's unique experience would spread across the whole world of Pea Land, to peas who would end up joining Huey. While together, they would create a new way of life for generations of peas to come.

The Story of Huey Pea

Garland Thomas-Emmanuel Smith

© 2023

Content

Introduction

In Pea Land, there are peas. Peas in Pea Land interact with Human Land through farmers' markets. And peas in Pea Land created Econolights to enhance their Human Land interaction.

Chapter 1: Peas

In Pea Land, there are peas, and peas grow together in peapods. Peas in peapods are sensitive to levels of light, water, pests, root damage, and even peapod-related injuries. When peas are in their peapods, they are somewhat protected by the strength of the pods as they grow.

Peapods provide protection for growing peas, so that peas can mature in their pods without being affected by what they are sensitive to, until they have grown strong enough to no longer need their pods. When peas no longer need their pods, they leave their pods and, when peas leave their pods, this is called their maturity.

Chapter 2: Maturity

At maturity, when peas are strong enough to no longer need their pods, they venture out of their pods and embark on journeys around the world. Peas journey the world and interact with peas from different communities as they create joyous life experiences for themselves with each other.

There are many types of pea communities, all around the world:

Some are outdoor, while some are indoor,

And some are in the mountains, while others are at sea level,

And there are a whole lot of pea communities that lie somewhere in-between.

"There are many types of pea communities, all around the world:

4

While some are in the

mountains,

and some are at

sea level,

And there are a whole lot of pea communities in-between."

When peas journey the world and have their most joyous experiences with peas they meet from different communities, they realize from their memories that some experiences were more joyous than others. When peas realize they remember their most joyous experiences from all of their travels, like a beautiful collection of experiences, it is when peas want and are ready to be sacked. The wanting and readiness by a pea to be sacked at the end of their journeying shows that they have arrived at the end of their maturity. Peas want and are ready to be sacked upon realizing they remember their most joyous experiences because, peas believe that after they are sacked, they live the remainder of their existence with the memories they held just before their sacking.

Chapter 3: Sacking

Being sacked—or sacking—is how peas end their maturities after journeying around Pea Land. When a pea is ready to end their journeying around Pea Land, they are sacked and sold for human consumption in Human Land. This is how life has always been for peas. Peas have always wanted to be sacked and sold for human consumption in Human Land, because that is what completes the mission of peas. The mission of peas is to journey around the world of Pea Land and create joyous life experiences with each other until their sackings, for which they are sold together in sacks for the most profit they can earn for Pea Land.

Being sacked and sold is competitive for all peas in Pea Land, because peas are not the only food consumed by humans in Human Land. Peas compete with other foods for sale in Human Land, so peas try to outcompete other foods for sale at farmers' markets between Pea Land and Human Land by creating the best sacks of themselves that humans will buy. The profits earned from the sales of sacks of peas are collected for the central treasury of Pea Land who uses the profits from the sacks of peas sold to maintain the evolved ways of Pea Land for generations to come enjoy Pea Land and create joyous experiences for themselves with each other too.

Over lifetimes, peas in Pea Land created systems of allocating peas into sacks to efficiently earn the most profit in selling themselves for human consumption, seeking to outcompete other foods for sale in Human Land. These systems of sacking evolved over pea lifetimes to reflect trends in recorded sacking systems in Pea Land that proved to create the most profitable sacks for sale in Human Land. Historically, pea communities would frequently argue with each other on deciding which sacking systems were the best to use across the whole world of Pea Land. Arguments were frequent, with pea communities accepting and refusing peas into sacks based on their beliefs of which sacking system would be best for earning the most profits. Until, eventually the majority of peas agreed on a solution for deciding the most profitable sacking system to use across all of Pea Land, so there would be no more arguments amongst peas.

The majority of peas agreed to delegate the responsibility of deciding the best sacking system to an independent authority that they would create together to serve all peas. The independent authority created together was a technology called "Econolight," and each Econolight would host a new delegated responsibility network for all Econolights to connect to and use for authorizing the allocations of peas into sacks to earn the most profit for the central treasury.

This new network hosted and shared by Econolights would use an algorithm that was programmed by uploading the records of trends in sacking systems over lifetimes which proved to create the most profitable sacks for sale in Human Land. The algorithm would update whenever an Econolight scanned peas to allocate them into new sacks, or whenever an Econolight recorded the profit from each sale of a sack. By each update, the algorithm would be continuously providing the most updated information on profitable sacking trends for all Econolights around the world to use when they connected to their network to allocate peas into sacks.

This continuously updating sacking system created using Econolights—as Econolights were exclusive hosts to use, maintain, and update the algorithm of their network—would eventually be referred to as the "Econolight system." Peas understood that the Econolight system earned profits in the most efficient way for the central treasury of Pea Land to use to maintain the evolved ways of Pea Land.

Chapter 4: Econolights

Every region in Pea Land had Econolights created to allocate peas into sacks at the end of their journeys, as peas would end their journeys in different regions with other peas, all around the world. Econolights were the technology and authority that peas in Pea Land delegated the responsibility of sacking to, as all Econolights would connect to and use a delegated responsibility network that had an algorithm to help them maintain a system of efficient profiting from sacks of peas sold in Human Land. Those profits from sales of sacks of peas were used for maintaining the evolved ways of Pea Land after peas were sacked and the new generation of peas emerged from their pods to journey around the world.

Most peas were satisfied with the Econolight system, because they enjoyed their journeys while experiencing the evolved ways of Pea Land, and they felt the new generations of peas would enjoy experiencing the evolved ways of Pea Land too. Peas also no longer argued about the most efficient way of sacking at the end of their journeys as the Econolight system operated, and because of this, joy levels of peas increased by relief that arguments before their sackings would no longer be memories that peas held just before their sackings.

Econolights maintained their system of allocating peas for sackings by shining their lights on peas, in a scan to appraise them. It was simple, by their network's algorithm, Econolights would shine their lights on peas and the light shined would immediately collect information about the pea for the algorithm to decide which sack around the world was best to allocate the pea into. This Econolight system was progressively becoming more efficient with each scan of peas and each sale of a sack of peas at farmers' markets, as each scan and update from a sale would change the algorithm with new information to recommend sacks around the world that would earn the most profit for Pea Land.

While the Econolight system was creating profitable sacks for Pea Land efficiently, it was eventually becoming apparent to peas that the algorithm the Econolights were using was providing information for Econolights to allocate peas into sacks based on their colors. Allocating peas by color was the most efficient profiting trend that the algorithm gave for Econolights to use, based on lifetime records and updates once the Econolight system began operating. It was unknown to peas when they created Econolights that, as Econolights only shined a light on peas to appraise them, the determining factor in the information collected would be the color of the pea. The Econolight system became a simple pattern of sacking and selling peas by color, but it was consistent—for efficiency—at selling sacks of peas which were sold at a standard price—for profit —for Pea Land to be maintained:

Sacks of green-hued peas sold at a standard price around the world,

Sacks of yellow-hued peas sold at a standard price around the world,

And sacks of brown-hued peas sold at a standard price around the world.

Even though the Econolight system used color as the determining factor for allocating peas for their sackings, nothing changed. The status quo remained, because peas already agreed on creating this system together so there would be no more arguing, and because it was creating profitable sacks for Pea Land efficiently. Econolights continued their system of sacking based on color.

Chapter 5: Huey Pea

Huey Pea was one of one trillion peas in the world, and would end up changing the lives of one trillion peas and more. Huey Pea, like all peas before maturity, was sensitive. When Huey was maturing in their peapod, a bird talon made a small cut on the outside of the pod, over the area where Huey was inside. This cut was severe enough, though, to allow more than normal levels of light and water into the pod that would affect Huey while they were maturing. So, when Huey Pea reached maturity, their color turned out to be more brown than others, even more brown than the peas in the same pod.

Like all peas, Huey Pea embarked on their own journeying around the world after maturity and, like other peas, met many great peas, as they all created joyous experiences in their journeying together. Huey was the same as other peas in Pea Land and no other peas that Huey met saw differently. Huey ended up having the best experiences with other peas and was living their best journey of maturity with joy, and this is how most peas were.

Journeying so much, as joyous experiences and great relationships were accumulating, Huey was reaching the end of their maturity. As Huey began remembering their life created, like a beautiful collection of experiences, Huey felt they were ready for their sacking. Huey was ready to join a sack in the region they were in and with the most joyous peas they met in their most recent experience. Many peas who Huey was with felt a perfect alignment together with Huey on being ready for their sackings too. So, Huey and the other peas, all remembering their joyous experiences and feeling they were at their maturities ready to be sacked, decided to go together to a sacking station in the region they were in.

All of the peas with Huey wanted to be sacked together in the same sack, so their joy together and the experiences they held in memories would not be interrupted in the process of being sacked and sold for human consumption. They all, like other peas, believed this was the best way to be sacked, so the most recent memories held would be what they remember for the remainder of their existence. They all felt ready for their sacking together upon their arrival at the sacking station, but when they tried to join a sack of their choosing, the Econolights at the station were not so inclined for them to be sacked together.

Econolights, of course, are not peas, and saw life very differently. Econolights did not journey the world having joyous experiences with each other like peas did. Econolights only worked to maintain a system for efficiently profiting from sacks of peas sold for the central treasury of Pea Land. So, when Huey Pea and the most joyous peas they met arrived together at the sacking station, Huey Pea was scanned and appraised by color and told by an Econolight that they could not join the sack with the other peas.

The other peas who Huey was with were mostly green-hued, while some were closest to yellow-hued, according to the Econolight system. While, according to the Econolight system, Huey Pea was very much a brown hue. The Econolight told Huey Pea that they were very much brown and that there was a better sack for them, because of their color, in another region not far away from the one they were in together. However, the sack that Huey Pea was told to join by the Econolight was not in a region nor

16

with peas that Huey remembered having their most joyous experiences.

Though it was common for appraised peas to be allocated by Econolights differently than where and with whom they desired, such allocated peas judged this way would go to where they were told by Econolights only contentedly, and not joyfully. When peas would follow judgment by Econolights contentedly, it was because they simply felt ready to complete their mission as peas and be sold in sacks for human consumption.

While, some allocated peas who were judged this way by Econolights would go to where they were told—not contentedly but—reluctantly, rather than joyfully, because those peas truly valued the joy they felt and were feeling they would remember in being sacked where and with whom they desired. Reluctant peas would feel that, by following judgment by Econolights, they would remember their sacking merely dutifully, rather than remembering their sacking as a joyous experience of completing their mission as peas.

Following judgment by Econolights contentedly or reluctantly usually interrupted the joyous memories that peas held as they were being sacked, as the judgment experience would create new memories that were not joyous for them. Huey Pea experienced these feelings of being judged and understood the reluctance in following the judgment by the Econolight. Acting on their feelings, Huey chose to do something different.

Chapter 6: Different

Thinking, "This is no way to be sacked," Huey would say to the Econolight who judged them, "No, I refuse, this is no way to go out." Huey then continued, "How can you tell me that I must now go somewhere else, after all my experiences of creating joy for Pea Land with other peas, and after thinking throughout my journeying that I can leave Pea Land with these joyous memories and peas with me? How can you tell me there is a better sack for me to join, with peas there who I have no memory of joyous experiences with? If I must do this, I will do it reluctantly and will now remember this experience for the reminder of my existence after my sacking, and that is unfair."

This is no way to go out, Huey confidently continued thinking, before lastly saying to the Econolight, "I do not consent to being sacked and sold elsewhere, I believe deeply that this is where and how my sacking is meant to be." Huey thought that by arguing with the Econolight, the memories they held before their sacking could be saved and not replaced by a reluctant experience, thinking the memory of arguing and being sacked in a joyous way was better than following the judgment by the Econolight.

Conversely to Huey's expressions, the Econolight replied, "Well, Huey, we run on a centralized network with an algorithm to appraise and allocate peas for efficient profiting, while the profits are used to maintain the evolved ways of Pea Land." The Econolight then questioned Huey's decision by asking, "Did you not enjoy the evolved ways of Pea Land as you said you did, and do you not want the evolved ways of Pea Land preserved for generations to come?"

The Econolight continued, "The network we connect to has an algorithm that is shared with all Econolights around the world of Pea Land. If you journey elsewhere, or try with another Econolight here, you will still be judged in the same way. You will not be able to join the sack you want here, but you can join a better sack that we have already discovered for you, with peas who look more like you, and where we will earn efficient profits for maintaining Pea Land." Although the Econolight explained that the judgment was for efficiently profiting from sales of sacks to maintain the evolved ways of Pea Land, Huey Pea stood firm in their decision and reiterated, "No, I refuse, and I do not consent to being sacked and sold by your judgment." Now, refusal is like pea self-imprisonment in Pea Land. Once a pea is scanned for allocation into a sack by an Econolight, the color of the pea is saved by Econolights into their network's algorithm that uses the collectively updated data from all scans across Pea Land to allocate peas. When the color of a pea is saved by the scan, it is almost impossible to change how the Econolight system sees you. This means that, since the color of Huey has already been saved into the algorithm of the Econolight system, Huey must either go to where they were told reluctantly and not joyfully, or Huey Pea would never be sacked and sold for human consumption, and would never complete their mission as a pea.

Huey Pea wanted the joyous peas and experiences to be the memories they held for the remainder of their existence, not the judgment by Econolights to just be sacked and sold with peas by a superficial appraisal for Pea Land profit. Huey Pea was worried, but tried to release the worrying thoughts. Soon after the rejection by the Econolight and upon realizing what refusal meant, Huey decided to leave the sacking station and search for opportunities to create more joyous experiences. It was the best thing Huey thought to do instead of worrying about the judgment. As soon as Huey was leaving the sacking station to search for opportunities to create more joyous experiences, a thought dawned within Huey. Huey spoke their thoughts and said to themself, "Well, I met a lot of peas in a lot of places around the world, and we had such joyous experiences. Maybe... maybe some of those peas are still out there. I know those places must still be out there!" Upon thinking about how many peas they met in regions around the world, the thoughts developed into a plan for Huey that would release all worries.

Huey Pea contacted many peas whom they knew and thought would still be out in the world journeying, and many were! Huey explained to the peas what they felt about being judged to join a sack, and how they refused the judgment. Like how Huey was changed after the sun shined on their peapod as they were growing, the minds of the peas Huey contacted would change after Huey shared their story with them as they were journeying around Pea Land. The peas contacted by Huey empathized with the story, and shared the same feelings. Many who were contacted decided to travel to join Huey, so they could all create more joyous experiences together, while they would all avoid their sackings with Huey.

Not long after Huey and the peas they contacted grouped and began interacting with other peas who were journeying too, the feelings shared by the group as initiated by Huey's story would spread more and more to peas around Pea Land. Peas who were not part of the original group began to join the group as they empathized with the sentiments of the group and did not want to experience a contented or reluctant judgment either. The feelings began to spread so much through interactions that the group grew to form a community of like- minded peas, who all agreed the joy of each other and their experiences created together in the joyous places where they were was better than being sacked and sold without complete joy. Huey and the new community of like- minded peas that emerged began to support the organizing of more communities around the world for peas who felt similar about Huey's story.

Before they knew it, they helped organize large numbers of like- minded pea communities around the world to experience joyous journeys longer and longer with other joyous peas, while they avoided being sacked contentedly or reluctantly, or like Huey, not being sacked at all. Some peas in these new like-minded communities were eventually sacked contentedly or reluctantly, as living without completing any of their missions was becoming harder to maintain. These peas eventually chose to be sacked contentedly or reluctantly from feeling that they were not contributing value to Pea Land with the profit they would contribute by being sacked and sold for human consumption.

Many of these peas who were part of the new like-minded communities and who were eventually sacked would tell Huey before their sackings a similar story. They would say something to Huey like, "we are so happy to experience more joy with our new communities using the idea you began, but we must now go to complete our missions, even though we are not happy to do what the Econolights say is better for us. It is better for the ways of Pea Land to be maintained for the next generation."

Huey heard many stories like this, and would not argue with the peas. Huey would only be thankful for their sharing. Until, one day, Huey was overcome with sadness when hearing this type of story from a pea who was in the original group of peas with Huey. One of the peas Huey felt closest to, and one of the peas Huey first contacted too, decided to no longer be with their community that formed from the original group and was leaving to be sacked and sold by Econolight judgment. Overcome by deeply distressful feelings, Huey also deeply remembered the power of reaching for more joy when encountering sadness or worry. The power of reaching for more joy is how Huey overcame the worry they felt when judged by the Econolights before. Now, since Huey felt sad and worried about the sustainability of the communities they helped organize, because peas were still eventually being sacked and sold contentedly and reluctantly, Huey reached for more joyous thoughts.

Huey excitedly thought about new ways to help other peas and themselves avoid being sacked and sold contently or reluctantly, rather than joyfully. Huey thought deeply, bouncing from one thought to the next, until a most joyous idea came that they would choose! Huey thought, "Well, we have so many peas in these new communities. Actually, so many that we probably have enough joyful peas together to sack ourselves. And sell ourselves for human consumption!" So, that is exactly what Huey planned to do, starting with their community.

Chapter 7: Community

Huey shared their new idea with their community, to sack and sell themselves for human consumption, with the plan to start with the peas in their own community. The idea briskly sparked interest among the like- minded peas in the community, and like a spark to a wildfire, the idea spread to the other like-minded communities that formed around the world.

The idea reached the communities that Huey and their community helped organize, as they avoided being sacked and sold contentedly or reluctantly by Econolight judgment. Like wildfire spreads, consumes, and goes away leaving nothing but evidence to show it was there, the idea spread so fast that some communities of peas around the world actually sacked and sold themselves while leaving profit behind for Pea Land, before Huey Pea and their community even knew it would work!

When it worked for these communities, the success stories of the self-sackings and sellings were shared around the world. Their stories revealed that their sacks were immediately competitive with Econolight sacks, which explained how they were sold so quickly. Most of these new self-sackings and sellings even earned more profit than the same amount of sacks sold by the Econolight system. And with the profits these communities earned, the peas chose not to give it to the central treasury, knowing the profits would fund Econolight maintenance and new production of Econolights to maintain the Econolight system and the status quo.

Instead, the peas decided to start a new fund with the profits and they wanted the fund to be used to build a new cooperative system for self-sacking and selling that could serve all peas in Pea Land like themselves. The fund grew with each like-minded community contributing to the fund with their self-sackings and sellings, until the new cooperative system that the peas wanted was built, with the communities now being recognized as member communities of the cooperative system. The new member communities called their cooperative system the "Huepod Society Cooperative." After its formation, the profits from the self- sackings and sellings by member communities were then used to fund development and maintenance projects for continuing to evolve the ways of Pea Land with opportunities to create joyous experiences for generations, just like the central treasury of Pea Land.

The mission of this new cooperative system was developed and shared by Huey Pea and the peas in their community in founding documents, just before they decided to self-sack and sell themselves too by this new working system. The mission stated: "Although we do not agree with the Econolight system, we believe their process is neither right nor wrong. We do not hate their ways, we only have found more love in our new ways, and with this new love, we created a Huepod Society Cooperative (HSC). The bylaws of our new HSC state that, as long as you find joy amongst others, you may join a sack by one of our member communities, or create your own member community for sackings. The profits from the self-sacking and selling by your member community will be used to fund new projects and maintenance of Pea Land that preserve and evolve the ways of Pea Land and serve the next generations of peas who reach their maturities. This will allow peas to continue their journeys around the world, enjoy more experiences and for longer, until they feel ready for their sackings too, while holding great memories with communities they found joy in joining."

In the first year of Huepod Society Cooperative after being established and having recognized member communities across the world of Pea Land, member communities of the new cooperative system earned more profits by sales of sacks than the profit of the same amount of sacks sold by the Econolight system.

Chapter 8: The Market

The member communities of the new Huepod Society Cooperative were profiting more from their sacks sold than the sacks of peas being sold with the Econolight system. Flustered and curious, some Econolights decided to band together and venture away from their sacking stations to investigate how it was possible that their system that worked so well for so long, and that peas even created to operate for them, was now profiting less than the Huepod Society Cooperative.

These Econolights decided they would conduct research on farmers' market days, where sacks of peas were sold between Pea Land and Human Land, in search of data they could find to explain this phenomenon. All that the Econolights witnessed were humans buying the Huepod Society Cooperative sacks before their own sacks and for more profit, but nothing to explain why this data was coming.

The Econolights thought it was a hoax, a manipulated strategy by Huey Pea. But Huy Pea was gone, and the Huepod Society Cooperative was becoming too large and was earning too much profit for a hoax to be the explanation, they realized. It was a real and legitimate competition to their system, while their sacks were steadily profiting less than the Huepod Society Cooperative system. So, the Econolights continued their search for data to explain this phenomenon, as they also sought for ways to replicate the Huepod Society Cooperative profits so they could compete with them more and maintain their Econolight system.

At a market one day, as the banded together Econolights were leaving after another day where their sacks sold for less and sold last, they stumbled upon a newspaper article on the ground. The article's headline stated: "Newfound brown, yellow, and green pea sacks!" While the article's subheading stated: "They are not only beautiful and joyous to cook and consume, they make you feel better too!" The Econolights read the whole article and found out that humans preferred buying peas of different colors together in a sack more than buying peas that were separated by color in different sacks. When cooking, the different colors of peas together seemed to produce a more vibrant scent, and the different peas looked great together when they were cooking and after they were cooked. The scent and look were amazing to humans when the peas were diversely combined, and humans felt better after consuming these peas too, which humans thought was a placebo effect from enjoying the smell and sight of the peas when cooking and eating them. These feelings were so noticeable to humans that the Huepod Society Cooperative member communities were profiting much more by their sacks sold than the gradually failing Econolight system of sacking peas based on color.

After the banded together Econolights read the article and the news spread from Econolight to Econolight, Econolights around the world viewed the Huepod Society Cooperative with a new perspective about why their Econolight system was being outcompeted. With a more descriptive perspective provided by the article, Econolights around the world began to realize that the Huepod Society Cooperative peas were actually more plump in size, stronger on the outside, and more vibrant in color compared to the peas of like-hues being sacked by the Econolight system. Econolights soon understood that their network's algorithm, that was efficiently allocating peas based on color, was to blame for their failing system.

Chapter 9: A New Way

What the Econolights found out from reading the newspaper article at the farmers' market, about why they were being outcompeted by the Huepod Society Cooperative,spread across the whole world of Pea Land from Econolights to peas. Beautiful chaos emerged that led to a worldwide transformation of Pea Land. Most peas who had any previous thinking to be sacked and sold contentedly or reluctantly by the Econolight system began to join Huepod Society Cooperative member communities instead. Or,they would organize their own communities with peas they had joyous experiences with and in regions where recognized Huepod Society Cooperative member communities were not yet created.

The collective consciousness of peas to transform their ways of sacking and selling was becoming so unanimous that, eventually the transformation of Pea Land from the centralized Econolight system to the new cooperative system transformed the direction of profits for Pea Land too. Instead of profits going to the central treasury, profits were channeled to member communities of the Huepod Society Cooperative. While now, as Econolights witnessed their system failing with losses in centralized profits to maintain their status quo, they were gradually becoming unable to fund their own Econolight maintenance and new Econolight production too. The Econolights were progressively becoming obsolete, but the beautiful technology that they were, as hosts of a network with an algorithm that worked consistently for so long, was not without avail.

One of the Econolights who banded together before and who read the newspaper article at the farmers' market still had the information from the newspaper in their storage. Now knowing hue was the determining factor of their network's algorithm, the Econolight attempted to upload the stored information from the newspaper to the algorithm like an update, to reprogram it so it would scan peas for more diverse factors than hue alone. The algorithm received the information uploaded and the successful attempt actually established a new and more diverse foundation of factors to determine how to allocate peas.

This was the first reprogramming of the algorithm since the Econolight system started operating when peas created Econolights, and it would overwrite the programming that founded the Econolight system. The Econolight thought this new programming could be an opportunity to revive their system so they could still provide service for Pea Land and earn profits to fund their own Econolight maintenance and new Econolight production. However, the Econolight had concerns about how to do this, because peas were already joining Huepod Society Cooperative member communities, instead of being sacked and sold by their Econolight system.

The Econolight knew, to try this new programming, they would need new scans of peas. So, the Econolight quickly went to where they knew peas were now grouping, at the nearest Huepod Society Cooperative member community they could find. They arrived at the first community they could find, with their plan on arrival to scan the peas at the community in an attempt to revive their failing Econolight system.

When the Econolight began scanning peas in the formed community where they arrived, the peas stopped what they were doing to ask what the Econolight was doing. The Econolight explained to the peas how they reprogrammed the algorithm with the information from the newspaper, so now their network's algorithm had a new foundation of factors to determine how to allocate peas. The Econolight continued explaining how this newfound ability to reprogram the algorithm could be an opportunity to completely redesign the Econolight system, so Econolights could continue providing service for Pea Land and earn the profits they needed so they would not become obsolete. Still, the peas did not want the Econolight system anymore, as they already created a new cooperative system they loved and enjoyed more. However, when the Econolight explained how they reprogrammed their network's algorithm with saved information, this new knowledge helped to finalize a great idea that all Huepod Society Cooperative member communities were already thinking about and designing.

Huepod Society Cooperative member communities were thinking about and designing an idea for all peas to find communities most joyous for them, as some peas were still being sacked and sold contentedly or reluctantly because they were not able to find or create a community that was joyous for them to join. To help all peas access member communities that would be joyous for them to join and be sacked with, Huepod Society Cooperative member communities wanted to create an accessible database to store descriptions of all member communities. Then, peas could use the database to find any member community around the world to join that would be joyous for them.

Back when the Econolight arrived at the first community they found and shared how they saved information from the newspaper, the peas in that community already knew how Econolights shared a network across the whole world. But now, as the new information from the Econolight combined with what they already knew, it was like the community found the missing piece to complete the idea they were thinking about and designing. The idea, now complete, was for each member community around the world to have an Econolight scan the peas in their community to store the information about the peas from each scan. And by scanning each pea only in the communities they joined, the scans of each pea consolidated together could create a description of what their community was like. With a description created for each member community around the world, the stored descriptions in Econolights could then create a database of all Huepod Society Cooperative member communities, as each Econolight shared the descriptions with each other around the world using their network.

Fortunately for Econolights too, as sackings could be done more efficiently and joyfully using the Econolights, member communities could share the profits they earn from their sackings and sellings with their Econolights, so Econolights could fund maintenance and new Econolight production as they need to not become obsolete.

Once the idea formed in the first community where the Econolight arrived, the community immediately contacted as many member communities around the world as they could, to share the idea that can help all peas. While, they requested that those communities contact more communities too, for the idea to spread and become as operational as possible. After a few communities were contacted, the idea spread like wildfire. As more and more communities adopted the idea, many communities began to call the newly forming database the "peachain network."

The peachain network formed across the world and began operating like a decentralized network of communicating and trading while making profit, in contrast to the centralized Econolight system and central treasury. The peachain network was saving each scan into Econolights like a transaction with a record of when the scan happened, so the most recent scans of peas who joined each community were used to determine the most updated description of what each community was like. Nonetheless, the peachain network worked efficiently, with each new record of a pea who joined a community immediately being consolidated into the description of what the community was like, for all peas around the world to reference. This efficiently helped all peas around the world find communities they would find joy in joining, while it also increased efficiency for each community to have the most joyous peas join them. The peachain network was revolutionary for Pea Land, as it easily helped member communities with newly joined peas create the best experiences together before they would be sacked and sold together, all while they held joyous memories throughout the process!

With this efficient and accessible peachain network for Huepod Society Cooperative, each member community began earning more profits than before, as sackings became easier and more joyous without any peas joining or being sacked reluctantly or contentedly anymore. Operations with the new peachain network continued with so much efficiency that finding a sack when a pea was at the end of their journey was never a concern anymore for peas in Pea Land.Peas would be told of this overcome worry from the moments they reached their maturities and left their pods to begin their journeys around the world. And while Econolights had enough profit to fund their own maintenance and new Econolight production now too, obsoleting Econolights was no longer a worry in Pea Land either. Now, joyous from the start of when peas left their pods to the finish of their journeys with their eventual sackings, Pea Land would experience an increase in total joy levels to a level of joy that was higher than any time in recorded history.

Chapter 10: After Land

Times of joy continued in abundance across Pea Land, and the continued sales of sacks by Huepod Society Cooperative member communities kept humans in Human Land happier and healthier too! But, the strangeness of the placebo hypothesis, in which humans thought the reason for increased energy levels were from the joy of buying and cooking the peas of different colors together, confused Human Land scientists, as there were just too many cases in Human Land where this hypothesis was the explanation.

Seeking to end their confusion, some Human Land scientists decided to try tests never done before on these new sacks of peas from the Huepod Society Cooperative member communities. The scientists would compare and contrast the new type of sacks of peas with the very last of peas in sacks made by the Econolight system, before they would stop circulating in farmers' markets. From their testing, the scientists found that the peas in Huepod Society Cooperative sacks were more plump, stronger on the outside, and more vibrant in color on average compared to the last of the peas sacked by the Econolight system. Something the Econolights in Pea Land already witnessed, the scientists in Human Land presented their wonderful discoveries, while knowing that energy is transferred from the foods that humans consumed into energy for humans after food is consumed.

"Eureka! Energetic peas," was the headline upon a new newspaper article that ran through farmers' markets to present the discoveries made by the scientists. Econolights, who happened to visit a farmers' market that same day to collect profits for their work from a Huepod Society Cooperative member community selling sacks, found the new article which presented the bold headline, "Eureka! Energetic peas." With much curiosity, the Econolights read the article in full and read where the article stated that, "New evidence has emerged on the phenomenon of pea sacks that are beautiful and joyous to cook and consume... and make you feel better too! It is evident that the peas are more plump, stronger on the outside, and more vibrant than the older pea varieties of similar colors that we used to purchase so much."

The article concluded, "There must have been one powerful pea seed that traveled the world and fertilized other pea farms with their own seed, and from that seed the new peapods matured to become more plump, stronger, and more vibrant than ever! Thank you, mother nature, thank you so much for this wonderful gift of new, joyous life!" Immediately from reading, the Econolights knew that Huey Pea was the powerful seed, or really the powerful pea who went around the world and generated energy amongst peas in Pea Land, which created Huepod Society Cooperative member communities who would sack and sell themselves in the most joyous ways.

That energy—that transformed Pea Land—created new generations of peas with more joyous experiences and more energy than ever before, and those high energy levels from joy in the peas which humans consumed would eventually transfer to high energy levels and joy for humans in Human Land! They laughed and said to each other, "Eureka!" Little did any pea know how much their energy helped humans. Barely even did many humans know how much energy was provided for them by what they consumed. While, after all was said and done, more than one trillion lives in Pea Land were changed, and years of life in Human Land forever more.

The End

The end.

Afterwords

Huey Pea might say, "Always reach for better thoughts like they are stars in your mind." Econolights might say, "Service is the rent paid for being in the world, profit by service." Humans might say, "Eat well, for food is your energy, and find joy in the processes of life." While the whole world might say to all, "Find joy in all that you do, and share joy with others."

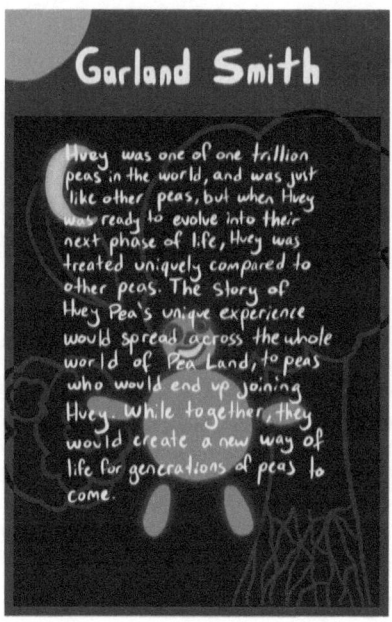

Garland Smith

Huey was one of one trillion peas in the world, and was just like other peas, but when Huey was ready to evolve into their next phase of life, Huey was treated uniquely compared to other peas. The story of Huey Pea's unique experience would spread across the whole world of Pea Land, to peas who would end up joining Huey. While together, they would create a new way of life for generations of peas to come.